The Baby Duck Stories

Amy Hest illustrated by Jill Barton

WALKER BOOKS
AND SUBSIDIARIES
LONDON • BOSTON • SYDNEY

First published individually as
In the Rain with Baby Duck (1995),
Baby Duck and the New Eyeglasses (1996),
You're the Boss, Baby Duck! (1997)
and *Off to School, Baby Duck!* (1999)
by Walker Books Ltd, 87 Vauxhall Walk
London SE11 5HJ

This edition published 2001

2 4 6 8 10 9 7 5 3 1

Text © 1995, 1996, 1997, 1999 Amy Hest
Illustrations © 1995, 1996, 1997, 1999 Jill Barton

This book has been typeset in OPTI Lucius Ad Bold.

Printed in Hong Kong

British Library Cataloguing in Publication Data:
a catalogue record for this book
is available from the British Library

ISBN 0-7445-8832-4

Contents

In the Rain with **Baby Duck**

Baby Duck and the New Eyeglasses

You're the Boss, **Baby Duck!**

Off to School, **Baby Duck!**

In the Rain
with
Baby Duck

Pit-pat.

Pit-a-pat.

Pit-a-pit-a-pat.

Oh, the rain came down.

It poured and poured.

Baby Duck was cross.

She did not like walking in the rain.

But it was Pancake Sunday, a Duck family

tradition, and Baby loved pancakes.

And she loved Grandpa, who was waiting

on the other side of town.

Pit-pat. Pit-a-pat. Pit-a-pit-a-pat.

"Follow us! Step lively!" Mr and Mrs

Duck left the house arm in arm.

"Wet feet," wailed Baby.

"Don't dally, dear.

Don't drag behind,"

called Mr Duck.

"Wet face," pouted Baby. "Water in my eyes."

Mrs Duck pranced along. "See how
the rain rolls off your back!"

"Mud," muttered Baby.

"Mud, mud, mud."

"Don't dawdle, dear! Don't lag behind!"
Mr and Mrs Duck skipped ahead.
They waddled. They shimmied.
They hopped in all the puddles.
Baby dawdled. She dallied and
pouted and dragged behind.

She sang a little song.

"I do not like the rain one bit

Splashing down my neck.

Baby feathers soaking wet,

I do not like this mean old day."

"Are you singing?" called Mr and Mrs Duck.

"What a fine thing to do in the rain!"

Baby stopped singing.

Grandpa was waiting at the front door.

He put his arm round Baby.

"Wet feet?" he asked.

"Yes," Baby said.

"Wet face?"

Grandpa asked.

"Yes," Baby said.

"Mud?" Grandpa asked.

"Yes," Baby said. "Mud, mud, mud."

"I'm afraid the rain makes Baby cranky,"
clucked Mr Duck.

"I've never heard of a duck who doesn't
like rain," worried Mrs Duck.

"Oh, really?" Grandpa kissed Baby's cheeks.

Grandpa took Baby's hand.

"Come with me, Baby."

They went upstairs to the attic.

"We are looking for a tall, green bag," Grandpa said.

Finally they found it.

Inside was a beautiful red umbrella.

There were matching boots, too.

"These used to be your mother's," Grandpa whispered. "A long time ago, she was a baby duck who did not like rain."

Baby opened the umbrella.

The boots were just the right size.

Baby and Grandpa marched downstairs.

"My boots!" cried Mrs Duck. "And my bunny umbrella!"

"No, mine!" said Baby.

"You look lovely," said Mrs Duck.

Mr Duck put a plate of pancakes on the table.

After that, Baby and Grandpa went outside.

Pit-pat. Pit-a-pat. Pit-a-pit-a-pat.

Oh, the rain came down.
It poured and poured.
Baby Duck and Grandpa
walked arm in arm
in the rain.

They

waddled.

They

shimmied.

They hopped in all

the puddles.

And Baby Duck sang a new song.

"I really like the rain a lot
Splashing my umbrella.
Big red boots on baby feet,
I really love this rainy day."

Baby Duck
and the
New Eyeglasses

B
A B
YDU
CKA
NDTH
EBADE
YEGLASS

Baby Duck was looking in the mirror.

She was trying on her new eyeglasses.

They were too big on her baby face.

They pushed against her baby cheeks.

And she did not look like Baby.

Baby came slowly down the stairs.
"Park time!" said Mr Duck. "Grandpa
will be waiting in his boat at the lake!"
"How sweet you look in your
new eyeglasses!" cooed Mrs Duck.
"Don't you love them?"

"No," Baby said.

"How well you must see in your
new eyeglasses!" clucked Mr Duck.

"Don't you like them just a little?"

"No," Baby said.

The Duck family went out of the front
door. Mr and Mrs Duck hopped along.
"Hop down the lane, Baby!"
Baby did not hop. Her glasses
might fall off.

Mr and Mrs Duck danced along.

"Dance down the lane, Baby!"

Baby did not dance.

Her glasses might fall off.

When they got to the park, Baby sat in the grass
behind a tree. She sang a little song.

"Poor, poor Baby, she looks ugly
In her bad eyeglasses.
Everyone can play but me,
Poor, poor, poor, poor Baby."

Grandpa came up the hill.

"Where's that Baby?" he called.

"I'm afraid she is hiding," Mrs Duck sighed.

"She does not like her new eyeglasses,"
worried Mr Duck.

Grandpa sat in the grass behind the tree.
"I like your hiding place," he whispered.
"Thank you," Baby said.

Grandpa peered round the
side of the tree.
"I see new eyeglasses," he
whispered. "Are they blue?"
"No," Baby said.

"Green?" Grandpa whispered.
"No," Baby said.

"Cocoa brown?"
Grandpa whispered.

Baby came out from behind the tree. Grandpa folded his arms. "Well," he said, "I think those eyeglasses are *very* fine."

"Why?" Baby asked.

"Because they are red like mine!" Grandpa said.

Grandpa kissed Baby's cheek.
"Can you still run to
the lake and splash
about?"

Baby ran and
splashed.

Then she
splashed harder.

Her glasses
did not fall off.

"Can you still twirl three times without falling down?"

Baby twirled.

One,

two,

three.

She did not fall down.
And her glasses did
not fall off.

"Come with me, Baby.

I have a surprise," Grandpa said.

They walked down to the pier.
Grandpa's boat was bobbing on the
water. There was another boat, too.
"Can you read what it says?"
Grandpa asked.
Baby read, "B-a-b-y."
The letters were very clear.

Then Grandpa and Mr and Mrs Duck
sat in Grandpa's boat. But Baby sat in
her boat and she sang a new song.

"I have nice new eyeglasses!
I look like my Grandpa.
My rowing-boat is lots of fun,
And I can read my name on it."

You're the Boss,
Baby Duck!

Baby Duck was having a bad day.

There was a brand-new baby in the house,

and everyone was making a great big fuss

for no good reason.

"What a fine little face," cooed Mrs Duck.

"Don't you love her little beak?"

"No," Baby said.

"What fine little feet," trilled Mr Duck.

"Isn't she hot stuff?"

"No," Baby said.

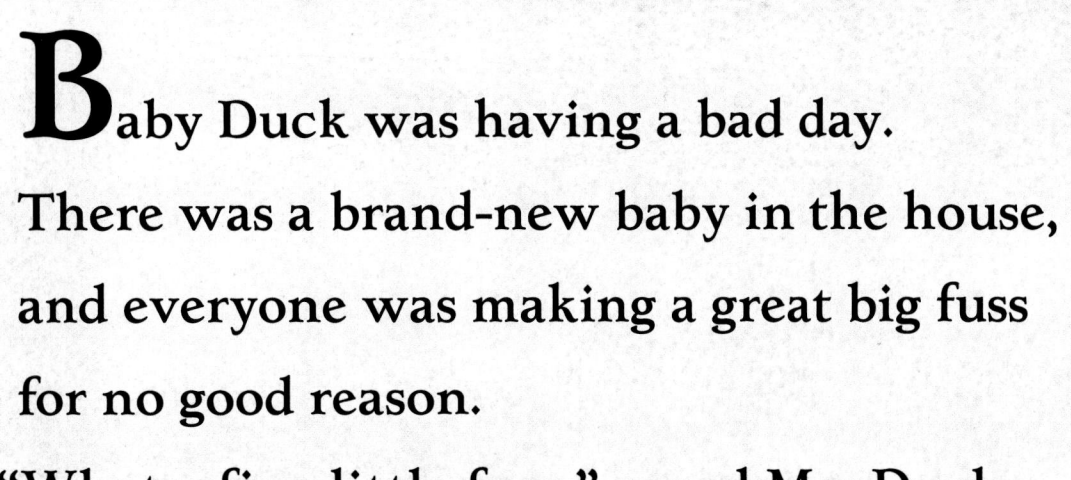

Baby Duck sat by herself. She sang a little song.

"Send that no-good Hot Stuff back,
No one wants her here.
Her beak is fat, her feet are fat,
And I'm the only baby."

"Are you singing to your baby sister?"
called Mr Duck. "What a fine sister you are!"
Baby stopped singing.

Baby got up and hopped on
one foot. "Look at me!"

Mrs Duck kissed Hot Stuff on her
fat little beak. She forgot to look.

Baby rolled over.

"Look at me!"

Mr Duck tickled Hot Stuff on her
fat little feet. He forgot to look.

Baby Duck turned
pages in her book.
"I can read,"
she said.

Mrs Duck put Hot Stuff into Baby's old coat.

Mr Duck tucked
Hot Stuff into
Baby's old
pram.

They did not hear her read.

"Time to show Grandpa your brand-new baby sister!" called Mr and Mrs Duck.

Baby Duck stomped along. She dragged her feet and mumbled.

"That bad baby is in my pram,
Wearing my nice coat.
I hope she goes away today
And stays away for ever."

Grandpa was waiting at the kitchen door.

He looked in the pram.

"Welcome," he said.

Then he kissed Baby's cheeks.

"Bad day?" he asked.

"Yes," Baby said.

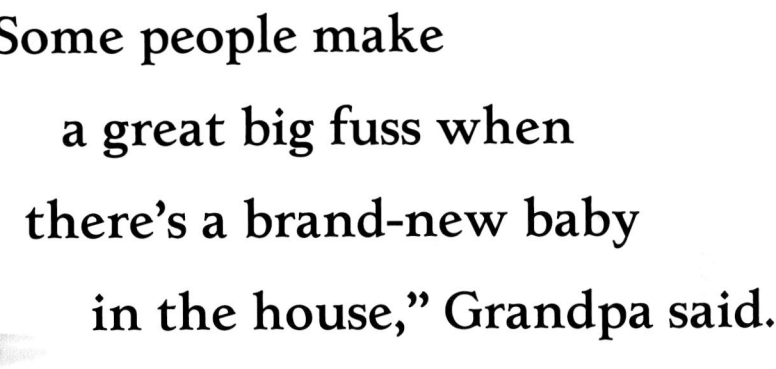

"Some people make
a great big fuss when
there's a brand-new baby
in the house," Grandpa said.

"Yes," Baby said.

"I am making lunch," Grandpa
said. "Want to help?"

"Yes," Baby said.

Baby Duck and Grandpa made lemonade.

Grandpa squeezed lemons.

Baby poured sugar.

"You are a good helper," Grandpa said.

"Brand-new babies are bad helpers,"
Baby said.

"Oh, yes," Grandpa said. "Brand-new babies
don't do much. They don't know how."

Baby Duck and Grandpa made sandwiches with jam. Baby fetched the bread. Grandpa chose some jam.

"Not that jam," Baby said. "*That* one."

"You're the boss, Baby Duck," Grandpa said.

"Yes," Baby said. "I am!"

The sandwiches were a big hit.

And, of course, the lemonade.

After lunch Baby put Hot Stuff
in her trolley.

"No crying," Baby said. "I'm the boss."

Hot Stuff did not cry.

"Look at me!"

Baby hopped on one foot.

Hot Stuff looked.

She gurgled.

"Look at me!" Baby rolled over.

Hot Stuff looked.

She burbled.

"Now I will read you a story."
Baby turned pages
in her book.

Hot Stuff gurgled. She giggled and
burbled and babbled.

After that, Baby Duck pulled Hot Stuff all round the garden. She sang a little song:

"Brand-new babies are a pain:
Fuss, fuss, fuss, fuss, fuss.
Maybe you can stay two days
But Baby Duck is boss!"

Off to School,
Baby Duck!

Baby Duck could not eat her breakfast.
It was the first day of school,
and her stomach was all jitters!
"Breakfast toast is very tasty," said Mrs Duck.
"Won't you have a bite?"
"No," Baby said.
"Breakfast juice is very juicy," said Mr Duck.
"Won't you have a sip?"
"No," Baby said.

"Your sister Hot Stuff is much too small to go to school," Mrs Duck pointed out. "She's not brave enough, either. Aren't you glad you're big and brave?"

"No," Baby said.

Baby Duck sat under the table
with her blue school bag.
Baby loved her school bag,
and the important things inside:
one favourite book,
a sandwich with jam,
one tall pad
and one yellow pencil
(a special going-to-school
present from
Hot Stuff).

"Button up your new school cardigan!" called Mrs Duck. "Hurry, Baby!"

Baby buttoned. It took a long time.

"Buckle up your new school shoes!" called Mr Duck. "Hurry, Baby!"

Baby buckled. It took a long time.

Mr Duck looked at his watch.
"Time to go!" he cried.

Mr and Mrs Duck bustled out of the front
door, swinging Hot Stuff in the air.
Their feet crunched on dry leaves.
"Come, come!" they cried.
"School, glorious school!"
Baby Duck dragged behind.
"Goodbye, house," she whispered
in a little small voice.

The Duck family waddled down the road.

"Hop to it, Baby!" called Mr Duck.

Baby could not hop. Her feet felt too heavy.

"Chin up, Baby!" called Mrs Duck. "Skip along!"

Baby could not skip. Her school bag was

bumping. *Bumpity bumpity bump.*

The Duck family waddled through the school

gate. Baby's buckle popped open and her shoe

started flapping. *Flappity flappity flap.*

"Calling all babies! Here I am!"
Grandpa was waiting on a bench.
Baby sat up close to Grandpa.
"Rough day?" he whispered.
"Yes," Baby said.
"Long walk?" whispered Grandpa.
"Yes," Baby said.
"Scared about school?"
whispered Grandpa.
"Yes," Baby said.
"Yes, yes, yes!"

"Sometimes it helps to sing a song,"
Grandpa said. "You sing nice songs, Baby."
"Yes," Baby said. "I do." Then Baby sang a song.

"Please don't make me go to school.
My teacher will be mean.
I won't have any fun or friends.
And who will buckle my new shoe?"

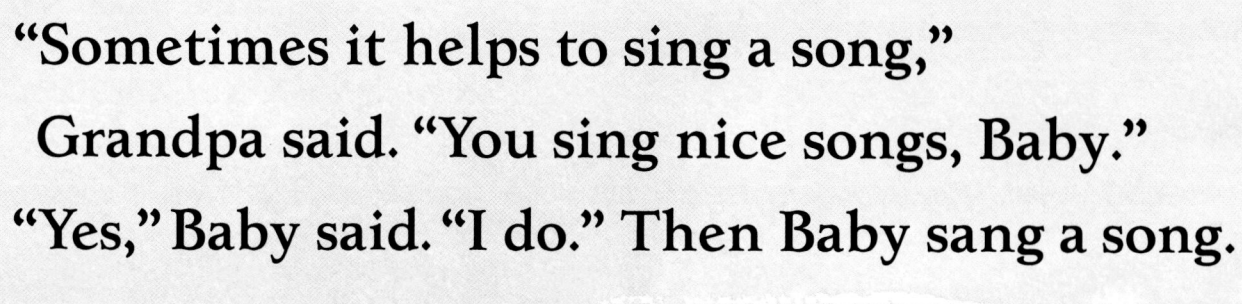

"I will," Grandpa said.
And he buckled Baby's shoe.

After that Baby showed Grandpa
the important things inside her school bag.
He liked the pencil from Hot Stuff.
"You draw nice pictures, Baby,"
Grandpa pointed out.
"Yes," Baby said. "I do."

Then Baby drew a picture.

Davy Duck took little steps towards Baby.

He looked at Baby's picture.

Baby felt proud.

Miss Posy came across the playground.

"My name is Miss Posy," she said.

"I'm the teacher."

"Are you mean?" Grandpa asked.

"Oh, no!" said Miss Posy.

"Do you sing songs in
your school?" Grandpa asked.

"Oh, yes!" said Miss Posy.

"Do you read books in there?" Grandpa asked.

"Oh, yes!" said Miss Posy.

"Do you like sandwiches with jam and yellow pencils?" Grandpa asked.

"Oh, yes!" said Miss Posy.

Miss Posy rang the bell. "Good luck," Grandpa said, shaking Baby's hand.

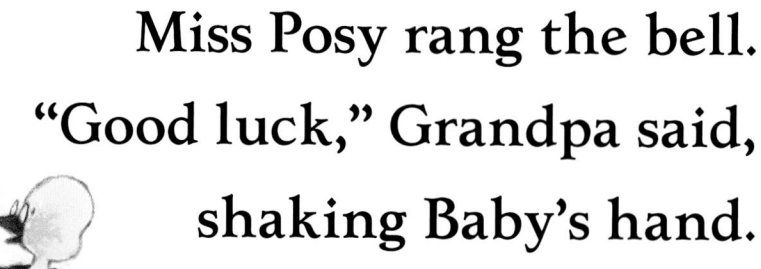

Then Mr and Mrs Duck took turns kissing Baby on both cheeks.

"We'll be right here," they promised, "when school finishes."

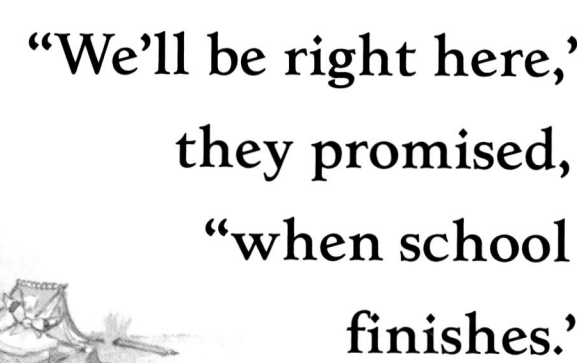

But Hot Stuff cried,
"Wa, waa,
waaaa!"

Baby Duck put her arm
round Hot Stuff.
"Little small babies have
to wait," she said.

She gave Hot Stuff
the picture she had
made. "Chin up!"
Baby called.

Then Baby Duck hopped and skipped up the steps to school with her new friend Davy Duck.

She sang a pretty song.

"Off to school, Baby Duck!
I am big and brave.
I like Miss Posy, Davy Duck too.
And I'll have fun at school!"